KEEP OUT

KEEP OUT

Fredric Brown

ÆGYPAN PRESS

Special thanks to Greg Weeks, Stephen Blundell, and the Online Distributed Proofreading Team (which can be found at http://www.pgdp.net).

This story was first published in the March, 1954, issue of *Amazing Stories.*

Keep Out
A publication of
ÆGYPAN PRESS

www.aegypan.com

With no more room left on Earth, and with Mars hanging up there empty of life, somebody hit on the plan of starting a colony on the Red Planet. It meant changing the habits and physical structure of the immigrants, but that worked out fine. In fact, every possible factor was covered — except one of the flaws of human nature. . . .

Daptine is the secret of it. Adaptine, they called it first; then it got shortened to daptine. It let us adapt.

They explained it all to us when we were ten years old; I guess they thought we were too young to understand before then, although we knew a lot of it already. They told us just after we landed on Mars.

"You're *home,* children," the Head Teacher told us after we had gone into the glassite dome they'd built for us there. And he told us there'd be a special lecture for us that evening, an important one that we must all attend.

And that evening he told us the whole story and the whys and wherefores. He stood up before us. He had to wear a heated space suit and helmet, of course, because the temperature in the dome was comfortable for us but already freezing cold for him and the air was already too thin for him to breathe. His voice came to us by radio from inside his helmet.

"Children," he said, "you are home. This is Mars, the planet on which you will spend the rest of your lives. You are Martians, the first Martians. You have lived five years on Earth and another five in space. Now you will spend ten years, until you are adults, in this dome, although toward the end of that time you will be allowed to spend increasingly long periods outdoors.

"Then you will go forth and make your own homes, live your own lives, as Martians. You will intermarry and your children will breed true. They too will be Martians.

"It is time you were told the history of this great experiment of which each of you is a part."

Then he told us.

Man, he said, had first reached Mars in 1985. It had been uninhabited by intelligent life (there is plenty of plant life and a few varieties of non-flying insects) and he had found it by terrestrial standards uninhabitable. Man could survive on Mars only by living inside glassite domes and wearing space suits when he went outside of them. Except by day in the warmer seasons it was too cold for him. The air was too thin for him to breathe and long exposure to sunlight — less filtered of rays harmful to him than on Earth because of the lesser atmosphere — could kill him. The plants were chemically alien to him and he could not eat them; he had to bring all his food from Earth or grow it in hydroponic tanks.

For fifty years he had tried to colonize Mars and all his efforts had failed. Besides this dome which had been built for us there was only one other outpost, another glassite dome much smaller and less than a mile away.

It had looked as though mankind could never spread to the other planets of the solar system besides Earth for of all of them Mars was the least inhospitable; if he couldn't live here there was no use even trying to colonize the others.

And then, in 2034, thirty years ago, a brilliant biochemist named Waymoth had discovered daptine. A miracle drug that worked not on the animal or person to whom it was given, but on the progeny he conceived during a limited period of time after inoculation.

It gave his progeny almost limitless adaptability to changing conditions, provided the changes were made gradually.

Dr. Waymoth had inoculated and then mated a pair of guinea pigs; they had borne a litter of five and by placing each member of the litter under different and gradually changing conditions, he had obtained amazing results. When they attained maturity one of those guinea pigs was living comfortably at a temperature of forty below zero Fahrenheit, another was quite happy at a hundred and fifty above. A third was thriving on a diet that would have been deadly poison for an ordinary animal and a fourth was contented under a constant X-ray bombardment that would have killed one of its parents within minutes.

Subsequent experiments with many litters showed that animals who had been adapted to similar conditions bred true and their progeny was conditioned from birth to live under those conditions.

"Ten years later, ten years ago," the Head Teacher told us, "you children were born. Born of parents carefully selected from those who volunteered for the experiment. And from birth you have been brought up under carefully controlled and gradually changing conditions.

"From the time you were born the air you have breathed has been very gradually thinned and its oxygen content reduced. Your lungs have compensated by becoming much greater in capacity, which is why your chests are so much larger than those of your teachers and attendants; when you are fully mature and are breathing air like that of Mars, the difference will be even greater.

"Your bodies are growing fur to enable you to stand the increasing cold. You are comfortable now under conditions which would kill ordinary people quickly. Since you were four years old your nurses and teachers have had to wear special protection to survive conditions that seem normal to you.

"In another ten years, at maturity, you will be completely acclimated to Mars. Its air will be your air; its food plants your food. Its extremes of temperature will be easy for you to endure and its median temperatures pleasant to you. Already, because of the five years we spent in space under gradually decreased gravitational pull, the gravity of Mars seems normal to you.

"It will be your planet, to live on and to populate. You are the children of Earth but you are the first Martians."

Of course we had known a lot of those things already.

The last year was the best. By then the air inside the dome — except for the pressurized parts where our teachers and attendants live — was almost like that outside, and we were allowed out for increasingly long periods. It is good to be in the open.

The last few months they relaxed segregation of the sexes so we could begin choosing mates, although they told us there is to be no marriage until after the final day, after our full clearance. Choosing was not difficult in my case. I had made my choice long since and I'd felt sure that she felt the same way; I was right.

Tomorrow is the day of our freedom. Tomorrow we will be Martians, *the* Martians. Tomorrow we shall take over the planet.

Some among us are impatient, have been impatient for weeks now, but wiser counsel prevailed and we are waiting. We have waited twenty years and we can wait until the final day.

And tomorrow is the final day.

Tomorrow, at a signal, we will kill the teachers and the other Earthmen among us before we go forth. They do not suspect, so it will be easy.

We have dissimulated for years now, and they do not know how we hate them. They do not know how disgusting and hideous we find them, with their ugly misshapen bodies, so narrow-shouldered and tiny-chested, their weak sibilant voices that need amplification to carry in our Martian air, and above all their white pasty hairless skins.

We shall kill them and then we shall go and smash the other dome so all the Earthmen there will die too.

If more Earthmen ever come to punish us, we can live and hide in the hills where they'll never find us. And if they try to build more domes here we'll smash them. We want no more to do with Earth.

This is our planet and we want no aliens. Keep off!

www.ingramcontent.com/pod-product-compliance
Lightning Source LLC
Chambersburg PA
CBHW030416310726
48979CB00002B/445

* 9 7 8 1 4 6 3 8 9 6 2 6 3 *